THE PUPPY PLACE

BITSY

THE PUPPY PLACE

Don't miss any of these other stories by Ellen Miles!

Angel
Bandit
Baxter
Bear
Bella
Bonita
Boomer
Bubbles and Boo
Buddy
Champ
Chewy and Chica
Cocoa
Cody
Cooper
Daisy
Flash
Gizmo
Goldie
Gus
Honey
Jack
Jake
Liberty
Lola
Lucky
Lucy
Maggie and Max
Mocha
Molly
Moose
Muttley
Nala
Noodle
Oscar
Patches
Princess
Pugsley
Rascal
Rocky
Scout
Shadow
Snowball
Stella
Sugar, Gummi, and Lollipop
Sweetie
Teddy
Ziggy
Zipper

THE PUPPY PLACE

BITSY

SCHOLASTIC INC.

For all my music-loving friends

Cover art by Tim O'Brien
Original cover design by Steve Scott

ISBN 978-1-338-21195-5

10 9 8 7 6 5 4 3 2 18 19 20 21 22

Printed in the U.S.A. 40

First printing 2018

CHAPTER ONE

"Please?" Charles Peterson pulled on his mom's sleeve.

"Charles Peterson, you promised you wouldn't beg me for things if you came shopping with me." His mom shook her head.

"I'm not begging," he said. "I'm just asking. Please? Can't we buy just one box?" He held up the cereal box and tilted it this way and that, trying to get her to admire the colorful package. "Look, it's vitamin-fortified! And it has six grams of protein."

"And sugar. Lots and lots of sugar." Mom pointed to some fine print on the label on the side of the box. "Not what you need at breakfast time." She shook her head again. "No way, my friend."

Charles gave up and trudged back up the aisle to replace the box. *My friend*. Ha! A true friend would buy you something you really, really wanted.

"Well, can I pick out some crackers, at least?" he asked, when he caught back up with Mom and her cart.

"Whole-grain, low-sodium," said Mom, without looking up from her list. "No added sugars or trans fats."

Charles rolled his eyes, but he knew better than to say anything. Mom was big on Healthy Eating Habits, and he was probably lucky she was willing to buy crackers at all. Next she'd be making him bake his own crackers, or eat peanut butter off pieces of cardboard or something.

"You can choose some biscuits for Buddy, too," Mom said. She tousled his hair and smiled at him. "Just make sure they're healthy ones. He shouldn't be eating junk, either."

Charles grinned. "He loves those salami sticks," he said. "They're his favorite."

Now Mom rolled her eyes. "Junk," she said. "Look for plain biscuits made with sweet potatoes or rice flour. He likes them just as much."

It was true. Buddy didn't seem to care very much what flavor or shape his treats were, as long as you kept them coming.

Buddy was Charles's adorable brown puppy. Actually he belonged to the whole family, but Charles liked to think Buddy was mainly his. They definitely had a special bond. Buddy loved to cuddle with Charles on the couch or in bed. He loved it when Charles threw his ball for him in the backyard. And he was crazy about the way

Charles stroked the heart-shaped white spot on his chest.

Buddy had first arrived in Charles's life as a foster puppy, along with his doggy sisters and doggy mom. All four dogs needed new homes. As a foster family, the Petersons had taken in many puppies, caring for them just until they found the right forever home for each dog. Buddy was tiny, the runt of the litter, and Charles had fallen in love with him right away. So had the rest of the family. It didn't take the Petersons long to realize that they were the best forever family for Buddy. He had been with them ever since.

Charles headed for Aisle 5: pet food, treats, and toys. It was one of his favorite places in the store—much more interesting than, say, the canned goods. Another of his favorite places to browse was the ice-cream freezer, but Mom obviously wasn't in the mood to buy goodies today.

As he passed the paper towels, a song came on the store loudspeakers and he started singing along. It was a really old song, about a girl with brown eyes, but Charles recognized it. He'd been listening to a lot of oldies ever since Dad had given him an ancient cassette player and some cassettes to go with it.

Charles had never seen cassettes before. They were little plastic boxes full of brown tape that had music recorded on it. The player and the cassettes were from Dad's high-school days. Some of the music was weird, but Charles loved most of it. Especially this one, with its "La la la-la la-la-la-la la-la-la la-di-dah" chorus.

"Charles!" someone called.

He turned to see who it was. "Mrs. Davies!" He grinned and waved.

Sometimes it was weird to run into grown-ups you knew from a certain place, like school, out in the regular world. Charles had once seen Mrs. Guzman, his school principal, in a shoe store. She was trying on a pair of sparkly blue high heels, and she seemed as embarrassed as Charles was when they spotted each other.

Mrs. Davies was different. She was sort of like a teacher—she had been the music director for a play Charles was once in—but Charles didn't feel weird around her, even in the supermarket. She was always jolly and warm, almost like a friend. She liked to call everyone "sweetie," and was always smiling.

"Hi, Mrs. Davies." Charles peered into her cart, curious about what she was buying. His mouth fell open when he saw that it was piled with boxes and bags of cookies. Chocolate cookies, peanut butter cookies, lemon cookies . . . all his favorites, in one place. All the things Mom refused to buy.

She noticed, and smiled at him. “I have a friend visiting for a while, and he has a sweet tooth,” she explained. Then her eyes lit up. “Hey, have you ever been in the Littleton Chorale?” she asked.

Charles shook his head. He’d attended their concerts, of course, just like everyone in Littleton. The community singing group gave four or five concerts a year in the town hall. The singers — all ages from kids to grandmas — were always enthusiastic and upbeat. Charles had always enjoyed their shows, but he’d never thought of joining.

“You should join us!” said Mrs. Davies. “Everybody’s welcome. This time my friend Mr. Craig is directing. He’s a retired music teacher and he lives in Kansas now, but he’s visiting me just so he can run the show. It’ll be a blast. For this concert all the songs are from movies and Broadway shows. And Mr. Craig is a lot of fun — you’d like him.”

"But—singing?" asked Charles. Singing alone in your room—or even in the aisles of the supermarket—was fun. Singing onstage was a whole other story.

"Sure," said Mrs. Davies. "You have a very nice voice. I remember from when we did the play. Plus, I heard you just now. You know how to have fun with a song. The chorus has been practicing for a while already, and the concert is coming right up, but with the experience you already have I'm sure you can jump right in."

Charles felt himself blushing at the compliment. He thought about the play he'd been in, which was about the history of Littleton. He'd been very nervous about being onstage, but a sweet foster puppy, a corgi named Cooper, had helped him through his stage fright. He didn't remember much at all about the singing part. "Really?" he asked.

Mrs. Davies nodded. "Think about it," she said as she pushed her cart forward. "We'd love to have you, and I think you would really enjoy yourself."

Charles thought about it as he picked out some blueberry-yogurt biscuits for Buddy. He thought about it as he chose some whole-grain crackers that he and Lizzie and the Bean would probably never eat because they were too boring. He thought about it while he and Mom were in line, and he thought about it as they carried their bags out of the store.

He only stopped thinking about it when he spotted a sign on the store's bulletin board, which was between the two sets of sliding doors.

ADORABLE PUPPY, it read. FREE TO A GOOD HOME.

CHAPTER TWO

"Mom!" Charles yelled. "Mom, wait!"

But it was too late. She had already pushed her cart through the second door and it was sliding shut behind her.

Without even thinking, Charles pulled the sign off the bulletin board and ran after her. "Mom!" he called, waving it in the air.

She was waiting for him by the soda-can return machines. She pulled two bags of groceries out of the cart and nodded to the third one. "Can you carry that?" she asked.

He held up the sign. "I will, but can you just look at this?"

"Charles," Mom said. "These bags are heavy. Let's get the groceries into the car, then you can show me."

Charles pulled the last bag out of the cart and followed Mom to the van. She slid the back door open and loaded her bags of groceries into the way-backseat. Charles got in with the bag he was carrying and buckled his seat belt, trying hard to be patient.

Finally, Mom got into the driver's seat. She turned around. "All right," she said. "What was it you wanted me to see?"

Charles held up the sign. "This," he said.

"Whoa, that is one tiny puppy!" said Mom.

Charles grinned. "I know. Isn't she the cutest puppy ever?" He turned the sign back his way so he could look at it again. The puppy in the picture looked a lot like Princess, a Yorkshire terrier the Petersons had once fostered: she had long silky brown hair, perky ears, and shiny brown eyes. The difference was in size. Princess had been a small puppy, and would probably never grow very large. But this puppy was smaller than small. This puppy was teeny-tiny, barely bigger than a hamster. In the picture she was posed next to a pink high-top sneaker. The sneaker had glittery pink laces.

Mom raised an eyebrow. "I wonder why she's looking for a new home," she said.

"I don't know, but we have to help her," said Charles. One look at this dog's picture had convinced him: she was the Petersons' next foster puppy.

"What do you mean?" asked Mom.

"We have to help her find a new home," Charles said, trying to be patient. "I mean, isn't that what we do as a foster family?"

"Well," said Mom.

"We can do better than a sign on a supermarket bulletin board," Charles said. "I know we can. We always find the best homes for the puppies we foster."

"Hmm," said Mom.

Charles thought that "Hmm" was a lot more encouraging than "well." He held up the sign again. "I mean, look at her," he said. "She needs us." The puppy in the picture did have a particularly pleading expression. Her shiny brown eyes seemed to say, "Won't you be my friend?"

Mom closed her eyes for a moment, and sighed. She handed Charles her cell phone. "I guess we might as well see what we can do, since you already took the sign off the board. Call your dad," she said as she turned back to start the car. "See what he thinks."

Charles wanted to burst out with a cheer, but he kept quiet. Better to make sure Dad was on board before he celebrated. He touched the picture of Dad on Mom's "favorites" list.

"Hi, honey," Dad said when he answered.

"It's not honey," Charles said. "It's me, Charles."

"You're my honey, too," said Dad.

Charles smiled. Then he told Dad about the tiny dog who needed a new home. "Mom says we can foster her if it's okay with you," he said.

"That's not exactly what I said!" Mom called from the front seat.

Dad heard her. He laughed. "Well, it's okay with me," he said. "A little dog like that can't be too much trouble, can she? It's not like she'll take up too much room, or eat us out of house and home like some of the bigger puppies we've fostered."

Charles giggled, remembering Boomer, the gigantic slobbery mess of a dog who had crashed into and out of the Petersons' lives. "I'm sure she'll be very easy," Charles promised. "And I'll do all the work."

"I'll remind you of that," Mom said, when Charles handed back her phone. She sounded stern, but she was smiling. Even though Mom always said she was more of a cat person, Charles knew that she got as excited as anyone else in the family when a new foster puppy was about to enter their lives.

Charles glanced down at the sign in his hands. So far he had only looked at the picture and the headline, but now he was checking for a phone number to call. He read the paragraph below the picture. "'Bitsy is a supersweet puppy, but she is not fitting in with our family. Can you give her the wonderful home she deserves?'" he read out loud. "Bitsy! I love that name. But I wonder what that means," he added. "Not fitting in with the family."

Mom pulled over at the next corner. “Well, I guess we should call and find out,” she said. “Read me the number.” She picked her phone up off the car seat and dialed as Charles read out the number.

“Hello?” she said. “I’m calling about the puppy you advertised. Bitsy?”

She listened for a moment, then frowned. “She’s not there?” she asked. “You mean you’ve already found her a home?”

CHAPTER THREE

Charles groaned. He looked down at the picture of Bitsy. He'd never even met her, but he already missed her. Was Bitsy going to be the foster puppy who never even came to visit?

"All right then, thanks," Mom said, after a moment. She hung up and turned to Charles.

"No puppy?" he asked.

She shook her head. "No puppy at that house. But we might still have a chance. That woman told me that Bitsy is just over at her sister's house. The woman's sister, not Bitsy's," she added, smiling. "But it's only temporary. Bitsy still needs a home."

Charles grinned back. “So can we go there?” he asked. “To the sister’s house?”

Mom punched some numbers into her phone. “Let’s find out,” she said.

Charles crossed his fingers. Maybe he’d get to foster Bitsy after all.

Mom waited, then started talking. “Hi, my name is Betsy Peterson. Your sister told me you’re taking care of her puppy?”

Five minutes later, they were on their way. Charles bounced in his seat, singing at the top of his lungs. *La la la la-la la-la la,* he belted.

Mom laughed. “Don’t get too excited yet,” she said. “We haven’t even met the puppy, much less decided to take her.”

“But I already love her,” said Charles. He picked up the sign and kissed Bitsy’s picture. He was just fooling around—sort of. He thought Bitsy was the cutest dog he’d ever seen, including dogs in books and in movies and on TV. A dog who could fit into a sneaker? Come on! What could be cuter?

In a little while, Mom pulled up in front of a small apartment building. "Unit 12," she said as she scanned the numbered doors. "I see unit 8, unit 10 . . ."

"There it is!" said Charles, unbuckling his seat belt. "See? At the end?"

They got out of the car and went to the door of unit 12. Mom knocked, and the door opened almost right away. A short blond woman smiled at them. "Hi, I'm Cecily. Come on in," she said. "Bitsy's waiting to meet you." She led them into her living room, which was full of overstuffed sofas and chairs that were in turn full of huge pillows. The furniture and the pillows were covered in big flowery prints.

Charles thought it was a little like being in a

giant's garden. He looked around for the puppy, but he didn't see her anywhere. "Where is Bitsy?" he asked.

Mom shushed him, but the woman laughed. "She gets a little lost in here," she said. "But at least she's safe."

"Safe?" asked Mom.

Cecily shook her head. "I don't know what my sister was thinking," she said. "She has three little boys and all they do is run around and wrestle and break things. A tiny dog like Bitsy wouldn't survive a week in that house." She nodded toward the couch, and Charles saw that she had made a little nest of pillows at one end.

"My sister loves Yorkies," said Cecily. "She had one before, and he was fine with the kids. But somebody at her job knew she'd lost her old dog, and gave her this puppy. The runt of the litter,

I'm guessing. She couldn't resist, but it didn't take long for her to see that Bitsy needed a different kind of home."

Now they were near the couch. Charles peered into the pillow nest and let out a long breath. "Oh!" he said. "She's even littler than I thought." The puppy was snuggled down between the pillows, looking like nothing much more than a tiny scrap of fur — except for her eyes, which sparkled back at Charles.

"Some people call dogs this size teacup dogs," said Cecily. "It's just kind of a made-up name, but they sure are tiny enough to fit in a cup. Anyway, this one is a Maltese-Yorkie mix. They call them Morkies. So I guess she'd be called a teacup Morkie."

Charles was barely listening. He held out a finger to Bitsy, and she reached up her tiny nose for a sniff. "Oh!" he said again. She was as tiny as the newborn kitten he'd once held at his cousin's farmhouse. "Can—can I hold her?"

Cecily nodded. "I can see that you're used to puppies," she said. "Not like those roughhousing nephews of mine." She gestured to the couch. "Have a seat."

Charles sat down next to the nest of pillows, and Cecily reached into it and picked Bitsy up. She handed the tiny puppy to Charles.

"Oh." Charles couldn't seem to stop saying that. "Oh, wow. She's so light! She doesn't weigh anything at all."

Cecily smiled. "She's a little thing, that's for sure. And a sweetheart. I've enjoyed having her here, even though I do sometimes worry that I'll sit on her by mistake."

Mom laughed. She and Cecily sat down across

from Charles and began to talk, Mom explaining about how their family fostered puppies.

Charles didn't hear a word. He held Bitsy up to his face and stared into her shiny brown eyes. He really was in love with her, no kidding around this time. "Hey, you little brown-eyed girl," he said. "Hey."

CHAPTER FOUR

Charles could not stop smiling all the way home. He still couldn't believe that it had happened—that his family was going to be fostering Bitsy. Mom had worked it all out with Cecily, and now Bitsy lay curled up in his lap as Mom drove. The tiny puppy seemed to trust him already, since she had fallen fast asleep by the time he had buckled himself in.

Charles stared down at the tiny dog. How could anything be so little? Her eyes were little, her nose was tiny, her paws were—oh! Those paws! Charles reached out a finger to touch one of Bitsy's feet. They looked just like regular dog paws, only miniature. "It's like somebody shrunk a dog," he said to Mom. "She's just so, so small."

Mom laughed. "I know," she said. "This will really be something new for us. We'll have to make sure that the Bean is extra-gentle with this puppy."

"I wonder what she eats," Charles mused. "Like probably one piece of kibble is a whole meal for her."

"I wonder what Buddy will think of her," said Mom. "Will he even understand that she's a dog, just like him?"

"Good thing he knows about being gentle, too," said Charles. Buddy was always great with their foster puppies. He shared his toys, didn't mind if they ate his food or drank out of his water bowl, and was always ready to play.

Charles looked down at Bitsy. *La la la la-la la la-la,* he sang softly.

She opened one eye and wagged her tiny tail.

That sounds nice! Do more.

Charles laughed. "I think she likes music," he said. "Or at least she likes my singing." He hummed a little more of the tune, and Bitsy sat up in his lap and wriggled happily. "Look at her!" he said. "She really does like it."

"I guess you and she are a good match, then," said Mom. "You've really been into music lately."

Charles remembered what Mrs. Davies had told him. "I forgot to tell you," he told his mom. "I saw Mrs. Davies at the store and she said I should join the Littleton Chorale for their next show."

"That sounds like fun," said Mom. "I've always wanted to do that. I love to sing, too. Maybe we could join the chorus together."

"Really?" asked Charles. "That would be cool." He'd never done anything like that with his mom.

"I'll call Mrs. Davies after dinner and find out more about it," said Mom. "But first . . ." She pulled into the driveway. "Let's get Bitsy settled in to her new temporary home."

Normally, the Petersons liked to let new foster dogs out into their fenced backyard. The dogs could run around and get used to the new smells, "do their business," and have their first meeting with Buddy outdoors, where there was more room to roam. But Charles could see that for Bitsy, the backyard would seem like a vast wilderness. She could get lost out there, maybe disappear beneath a rosebush and not be seen for weeks! He decided to keep her on her leash for the time being and take her inside through the front door.

"Come on, girl," he said. "Let's go meet everyone." He held her carefully as he got out of the van, then gently put her down on the ground. The rocks lining the driveway towered over her like giant boulders, and the front walk seemed as wide as a superhighway, but Bitsy did not seem fazed. She trotted along at the end of her little leash, wagging her teensy tail and sniffing at the ground—just like a regular dog. She even squatted and peed on a tiny clump of grass. "Good girl!" Charles said. He bent way down to give her a gentle pat.

When they got to the front steps, Bitsy stopped for a second to gaze at the sheer cliff in front of her. She turned to look up at Charles.

A little help, here?

Charles laughed. Of course! The stairs, so easy for Buddy to bound up, were way too high for tiny Bitsy. He scooped her up and held her close to his chest as he climbed the stairs and opened the door.

Buddy came galloping toward him for his usual happy greeting, but Charles stepped back. "Uh-uh, Buddy," he said. "Easy, boy. Sit. Wait till you see what I have here."

Buddy sat down and thumped his tail eagerly as Charles came inside and put Bitsy down on the floor. Bitsy looked up at Buddy, her brown eyes sparkling.

Hey, big boy! Let's play!

Buddy looked like a giant next to Bitsy, but he was a gentle giant. He stretched out his neck and the two dogs touched noses. Bitsy sniffed him, then went into a play bow with her tiny paws outstretched in front and her tiny butt in the air. Then she took off, skittering across the wooden floors of the hall and tearing into the living room with Buddy galumphing along behind her.

Bitsy ran straight for the basket full of dog toys. She leapt at it, didn't quite make it, leapt again, and jumped right in. Charles cracked up. Bitsy looked like a toy herself, sitting there surrounded by all of Buddy's well-worn playthings.

She opened her tiny mouth and grabbed at Mr. Duck, the most well-worn of all, then tried to shake the toy just like a big dog would. Mr. Duck was so much bigger than Bitsy that the toy barely moved, but Bitsy didn't seem to care. She just wagged her tiny tail and growled her tiny growls, and Charles could tell that she already felt right at home.

CHAPTER FIVE

Me may my mo moo, Charles sang. He wanted to giggle because the words sounded so silly, but everyone around him was singing the same syllables—and nobody else was laughing.

"Good! Next, start on this note," said the man sitting at the piano. Mr. Craig was his name, and he was the chorus director, Mrs. Davies's friend. He struck a note, higher than the note before, and everyone sang the same nonsense syllables on that pitch. *Me may my mo moo,* they chorused.

Charles looked over at Mom and raised his eyebrows. She smiled and shrugged, mouthing the words along with everyone else. She and Charles had both been nervous as they drove to their first rehearsal, but they had decided to give it a chance and see how they liked it.

The Littleton Chorale was a whole new thing for Charles, but so far it turned out that he liked it a lot. Mr. Craig was funny and nice, the other singers were helpful and friendly, and even though they had only begun warming up, Charles was enjoying the singing. The only bad part was missing Bitsy, who was home with Lizzie and Dad and the Bean.

Charles knew Bitsy was getting plenty of attention, since the whole family was crazy about her, but he hated to miss any time with her. Everything Bitsy did was funny and different, from the way she barked (she sounded like a squeaky toy) to the way she drank (she lapped up water one drop at a time from a tiny bowl Mom had filled). She had settled in nicely, and she loved the little bed Charles had made for her out of a shoebox lined with one of his oldest, softest T-shirts. Charles could picture her now, snuggled into her bed. Did she miss him like he missed her?

Me may my mo moo, sang Mr. Craig, playing an even higher note on the piano. The chorus followed along, singing with him. Then he went down the scale, playing each note on the piano as the chorus sang. "Great," he said, when they finished. "Now you're all warmed up and ready to sing, right?"

"Right!" everyone yelled.

Charles liked how enthusiastic the singers were. They were all ages, from kids even younger than him to gray-haired grownups much older than Mom. The only thing they had in common was their smiles. Charles could tell that everyone in that room really loved to sing.

"We'll start with a song that everybody knows," said Mr. Craig. "Let's sing it together, first. Then we'll divide it up into parts and try some harmony. Do you all know what harmony is?"

Charles looked around. Everyone was nodding. Everyone but him.

Mr. Craig must have noticed. "Harmony is when one person sings on a note a little higher or lower than the note another person is singing," he explained. "The two notes blend together in a way that can sound really nice."

"Or not, if you hit the wrong note like I always do!" called out a man near Charles, and everybody laughed.

Charles was beginning to realize that he had a lot to learn about music. That became even more clear when Mr. Craig passed out some printed sheets for the song they were about to sing.

When Charles had sung in the play, Mrs. Davies had handed out papers that just had the words to the song. This time, the sheets had a lot more than words. They had lines drawn across them, and oval black marks marching up and down the lines, and lots of other marks and squiggles that Charles couldn't make sense of.

He looked over at Mom. She smiled. *Don't worry*, she mouthed.

"Don't worry if you don't know how to read music," said Mr. Craig, practically at the same moment. "Just follow along with the words. Listen to your neighbors standing next to you, and try to get a feel for the way the song goes. That's all we're doing right now."

Charles looked at the title at the top of his sheet. "Do-Re-Mi" it said. He knew that song! It was from one of Mom's favorite movies, *The Sound of Music.* He'd watched the movie with her so many times that he'd memorized all the songs. Maybe this wasn't going to be so hard after all.

"Ready? One, two, three." Mr. Craig struck a chord on the piano and the chorus began to sing.

Charles sang along with everyone else. Mr. Craig smiled and nodded encouragingly as his long fingers raced over the piano keys.

Charles grinned as he sang. He liked hearing all the other people singing around him. This was really fun!

At the end of the song Mr. Craig lifted his hands off the piano and applauded. "Terrific," he said. "You all sound just wonderful. Now, let's try it again, with a little harmony. Altos, you'll lead us off with this melody." He played some notes on the piano and sang along. "Then the tenors will come in with this line," he said, and played different notes.

Charles froze. Altos? Tenors? He had no idea what those words even meant.

"And if you don't know what I'm talking about, just keep singing and see me after rehearsal," Mr. Craig said as if he was reading Charles's mind. "We'll figure out where you fit in."

Charles followed Mr. Craig's directions and did his best to keep singing. By the end of rehearsal, he was worn out and ready to go home to Bitsy. But Mom grabbed him and brought him up to see Mr. Craig.

"Mrs. Davies told me to expect you two," said Mr. Craig. "Welcome. I hope you had fun."

"I did," said Charles. "But I don't understand about the notes and harmony and tenors and altos and stuff."

Mr. Craig laughed. "Music is a whole other language," he said.

That was it! Exactly. Another language. There was something about those little black marks and squiggles that made Charles very curious. It was like when he learned to read books. At first, the letters didn't mean anything. Then, magically, they had become words. Suddenly, Charles wanted to learn to read music the same way he had learned to read letters. "I'd like to learn," he said.

Mr. Craig smiled. "When I was your age," he said. "I took piano lessons and learned to read music. It was the best thing that ever happened to me. Would you like me to teach you?"

Charles looked at Mom. She nodded.

"Yes, I would," he said.

CHAPTER SIX

"Where's Bitsy?" Charles asked. Then he asked again, more urgently. "Where's Bitsy? Let's find her!"

Fortunately, Bitsy was not actually lost. Charles knew exactly where she was, so he wasn't in the least bit worried. He was just trying to get Buddy excited about finding the tiny pup. It was the day after Charles's first chorus practice, and he had discovered something wonderful: Bitsy was the best hide-and-seek player ever! She could tuck herself into the tiniest corners and slide into the smallest spaces. Plus, she seemed to understand the game right away, and always stayed quietly in her spot until Buddy sniffed her out. Then she would pounce out of hiding, barking her squeaky-toy bark, and dash around the room with Buddy chasing after her.

Buddy snuffled and sniffled his way around the living room, trying some of the places where Bitsy had hidden before: the toy basket, where she had disappeared amidst the jumble of Buddy's favorite playthings; the couch, where she'd squeezed between two pillows until only the bow on top of her head was showing; one of the pockets in Charles's cargo pants; and the magazine basket, where she'd snuggled down into a pile of newspapers and catalogs.

No Bitsy. Buddy sat back on his haunches and stared up at Charles, as if he was hoping for a hint. Charles shrugged and shook his head, trying not to look toward the entryway by the front door, where Bitsy sat hiding inside one of Lizzie's daisy-patterned rain boots. Charles had helped her into it.

Buddy must have read his mind. He got up and trotted toward the front hall, snuffling and sniffing as he went. As he neared the line-up of shoes and boots by the door, he snuffled harder and harder. He approached the rain boots and stuck his nose into one of them—just as Bitsy popped out of the other! She barked her squeaky-toy bark and tore off down the hall.

Hee, hee! I win again!

Buddy pulled his nose out of the boot just in time to see Bitsy scamper off. Charles had to laugh at the expression on his puppy's face. Buddy looked like, "Hey, wait a minute, there. What just happened?"

"Charles," Mom called from her upstairs office. "It's almost time for your piano lesson. Better make sure you're all ready to go."

Charles groaned. When Mr. Craig had suggested piano lessons, Charles had been excited. Now he realized that the lessons were going to take up precious Bitsy time. He could hardly stand to miss one minute with that miniature bundle of fun. Charles knew that this foster puppy was not going to be staying long. She was too adorable! Somebody was going to scoop her up soon and adopt her. Charles thought Buddy would probably miss her as much as anyone in the family. The two puppies had become best friends in no time.

Buddy and Bitsy. Why couldn't they be BFFs? Charles wondered if he could convince his parents to adopt Bitsy. She was so small that they would hardly even know they had a second dog.

Dad was crazy about her, and so were Lizzie and the Bean. If Mom agreed . . . Wouldn't that be awesome?

"Charles, it's time to go. Grab your jacket." Mom came trotting down the stairs.

Reluctantly, Charles stood up and pulled on his jacket.

"Don't look so sad," Mom said, smiling. "We'll be back in an hour or so and Bitsy will still be here, waiting for you."

As they drove to Mrs. Davies's house, Mom chattered about how exciting it was that Charles was going to learn to play piano. "I always wanted to learn, too," said Mom. "But somehow it never happened. Maybe I'll pick up some tips from you. If we both decide we really like it, maybe we can find a used piano to buy."

Charles nodded and smiled, but he couldn't stop thinking about Bitsy. What was she doing right now? Lizzie had promised to keep an eye on her. Were they still playing hide-and-seek? He wondered where she might be hiding. In the potted fern by the fireplace? Behind the curtains? On the bookshelf? Bitsy could fit just about anywhere.

"Welcome!" said Mrs. Davies, when they arrived. "Mr. Craig is waiting for you in the living room." She waved Mom and Charles inside and took their jackets. Charles looked around. He'd never been in Mrs. Davies's house before, but he liked it right away. It was bright and cozy and warm. Mrs. Davies pointed Charles toward the living room while she and Mom headed for the kitchen.

"Hi, Charles," said Mr. Craig. He held out his hand for a shake. "I'm so glad you came. Before we play the piano I thought we could sit down for a few minutes and talk about music." He showed

Charles to a big comfy chair near the shiny black piano and passed him a plate piled with cookies. "Mrs. Davies spoils me when I visit," he said with a wink and a smile.

Mom was already in the kitchen chatting with Mrs. Davies, and Charles told himself it would be very rude to interrupt them just to ask if it was okay for him to have a cookie. He picked out one with peanut butter creme sandwiched between two peanut butter cookies. Yum.

Mr. Craig sat down next to Charles and opened a tattered old music book. The cover was red and white, and the book's title was, *Teaching Little Fingers to Play.* Charles looked down at his fingers, which already seemed to be holding a second peanut butter cookie. His fingers weren't so little, were they? They weren't long and thin like Mr. Craig's, but they were big enough.

"This book was mine when I was your age,

believe it or not," said Mr. Craig. Charles smiled as he tried to picture his teacher as a second-grade boy. He probably loved cookies back then, too.

Mr. Craig opened the book and began to talk about how music was made up of notes and how each note had a letter name. Charles listened and nibbled his cookie. He was already enjoying his piano lesson very much, even if it did mean giving up Bitsy time.

CHAPTER SEVEN

"Great Job, Charles!" said Mr. Craig as Charles picked out the notes. "See? You're already playing a song!"

Charles grinned up at him. This was fun. He was making music! The tune was really simple, but it was a tune. And Charles was reading the music and playing it, on Mrs. Davies's shiny black piano. He liked the way the glossy white keys felt under his fingers. There were black keys, too, and he knew that Mr. Craig was going to teach him all about them, but for now all Charles wanted to do was play the tune again. So he did.

"Whoops!" he said a moment later. He'd hit the wrong key, and it sounded terrible.

Mr. Craig nodded and smiled. "Don't worry about mistakes. My music teacher always used to say, 'If you're going to make a mistake, make it big. Then smile and move on.'" He pointed to the music book propped up on the piano, to the black notes that marched up the lines that went across the page. "The cool thing is that you *knew* you made a mistake. That means you have a good ear for music."

Charles felt his cheeks get warm, and knew he was blushing. "I do like music. And I like to sing," he said. "Especially with other people."

"So do I," said Mr. Craig. "It's the best. How about if we sing the song we worked on at practice? 'Do-Re-Mi'?"

"Sure," said Charles.

"And you can play the melody," said Mr. Craig. "That's the part most piano players use their right hands for. It's the way the song goes, like this. He sang as his long fingers danced over the keys. "The left hand is usually playing chords, like this." He played three lower notes at the same time with his left hand, making a sound that seemed to hold up the melody notes he was still playing with his right hand.

"Wow," said Charles. "I'll never be able to do that."

"Sure you will," said Mr. Craig. "It's not so hard. But we'll start you off just playing the top part." He played it again, slowly, so Charles could see which keys he was touching. "See? It's very simple."

They sat together on the piano bench. Charles played the keys that Mr. Craig pointed to. "Good!" said Mr. Craig. "Use your number one finger for that note." He began to play chords at the other end of the keyboard, and they began to sing as they played. They got all the way to the end of the song and went straight back to the beginning to do it again. "Yes!" said Mr. Craig as they came to the end. He held up his hand for a high five.

"Bravo!" called Mom. She and Mrs. Davies stood in the doorway to the living room, clapping their hands. "That's amazing," Mom said. "You can do that, after one lesson?"

Charles beamed.

"He's musical," said Mrs. Davies. "I could tell when he was in the play, and when I saw him singing in the supermarket the other day it reminded me. What was that song you were singing at the store, Charles?"

Charles sang a few lines. By the time he got to the "La-la-la la-la la-la-la" part, Mr. Craig was playing along on the piano. His fingers raced over the keys as they sang, doing fancy things that made the song better than ever.

They sang the whole song, getting louder and louder every time the "La-las" came around. Mom and Mrs. Davies were singing along, too, and Mom was even dancing a little. Charles's cheeks hurt from smiling so hard.

"I want to learn to play that song!" he said, when it was over.

Mr. Craig laughed. "You will," he said. "Once you learn to play piano you can play any song you want. Isn't that amazing?"

Charles and Mom sang the song all the way home, and he was still singing it as he walked into the house. Bitsy and Buddy ran over to greet him, and Charles plopped right down on the kitchen floor for hugs, still singing. Buddy ran off to get his toy—he always liked to show it off when people came home—but Bitsy climbed right up onto Charles's lap, ears alert as she gazed up at him. Her tiny black eyes sparkled and her teeny pink tongue poked out as she grinned a weensy puppy grin.

I love when you sing to me!

Charles gazed back down at Bitsy. "You're my brown-eyed girl," he said. "My music-loving brown-eyed girl." He shook his head, thinking about how much Bitsy would have loved hearing Mr. Craig play and sing. "Too bad you can't come with me to piano lessons," he told her. "I missed you today." He stroked her tiny head, remembering how cute she'd looked when she was hiding in the toy basket with only her bow showing.

"Hey," he said out loud. "Maybe you *can* come."

CHAPTER EIGHT

Charles sang out loud the next day as he played pretend notes on the kitchen table. He felt like his fingers were itching to play a real piano so he could hear the notes ring out as he touched the keys. For now, his imagination would have to do—at least until he went to his second lesson that afternoon. Maybe someday there would be a piano in his house, or even just a keyboard he could practice on. Wouldn't that be awesome?

Especially if Bitsy was still around to enjoy his playing. Charles had never met a dog who was so crazy about music! Whenever he sang or played a song on his cassette player, Bitsy was there at his side, gazing up at him and wagging her teeny-tiny tail. He looked down at her now. She was even excited about this silly little song. She put her paws up on his ankle and barked her squeaky bark.

More! Sing more!

"I promise you'll hear some good music today," he told her. He put his fingers to his lips. "But remember, it's our little secret."

He went on practicing. He wanted to show Mr. Craig that he was serious about learning piano. He wondered how long it would take before he could play the way his teacher did, dancing over the keys and playing any song he wanted.

"Charles!" called Mom from upstairs. "Your lesson's in an hour. Make sure you're ready."

"I will," Charles shouted back. He wanted to keep practicing, but there was something else he needed to do. For his great idea to work, first he needed to tire Bitsy out. "Ready for a game?" he asked her. "Hide-and-seek?"

She jumped up and spun around, squeaking happily.

I'm ready! I'm ready!

Charles scooped Bitsy into his arms and looked around the kitchen. "How about in here?" he asked, tucking the tiny pup into the bottom of the broom closet. He closed the door partway and called Buddy, who was snoozing on his bed in the living room. "Buddy!" Charles said. "Where's Bitsy? Find her!"

Buddy jumped up and ran into the kitchen. First he sniffed under the table. He checked the cabinets where the pots and pans were stored. He snuffled behind the trash can. All the time he was getting closer and closer to the broom closet. Charles could hardly keep from saying "Warmer, warmer, you're getting hot!"

Finally, Buddy sniffed his way to the broom closet. He pushed his nose inside, then used his paw to open the door wider. Bitsy jumped out, barking her squeaky bark.

You found me! Yay! Let's do it again!

They played until Mom came downstairs to take Charles to his lesson. By then, Bitsy had hidden in the big potted tree near the front window, under the couch, and behind Lizzie's science fair model of a salt crystal.

"Are you ready?" Mom asked. "I know it's a lot to go to piano lessons every day, but Mr. Craig isn't here for long so we might as well get there as often as we can."

"Ready," said Charles. "Oh—wait. I just need to grab my sweatshirt." Carrying Bitsy, he ran upstairs. When he came back, he was wearing his favorite sweatshirt over his cargo pants—and he wasn't carrying Bitsy.

Lizzie arrived home from her afternoon job walking dogs just in time for Charles to whisper in her ear. "Don't worry if you can't find Bitsy," he said as they passed in the kitchen.

Lizzie nodded. She'd heard Charles's plan the night before and she was all for it. She gave him a thumbs-up as he followed Mom out the door.

Charles's second lesson was a lot like the first. It started with cookies and talking—Charles liked that—but before long he was sitting next to Mr. Craig on the piano bench, playing "Do-Re-Mi."

"Excellent!" said Mr. Craig, when they got to the end of the song. "I think you've been practicing your finger movements. Am I right?"

Charles nodded, blushing.

"Let's see what else you can do," said Mr. Craig. He turned the pages of their music book to a song called "Baseball Days." "Try this one," he said.

Charles peered at the notes, and the numbers under them that matched the way Mr. Craig had taught him to number his fingers. He put his hands on the keys, fingers curved. And he played the song straight through.

"What did I tell you? You're a natural," said Mr. Craig. He struck a few chords and Charles recognized the chords to the song about the brown-eyed girl. Before Charles knew it, Mr. Craig was singing—and Charles couldn't help joining in at the top of his voce.

La la la-la la-la-la-la la-la-la la-di-dah, they sang together.

That was when Bitsy popped out of the pocket of Charles's cargo pants.

I know I'm supposed to be hiding, but I can't help it. That's my favorite song!

Charles tried to catch Bitsy and put her back into her hiding place, but it was too late.

Mr. Craig stopped playing. He stared at the tiny dog on Charles's lap. "Oh, my," he said. "Who might this be?"

Bitsy hopped up onto the piano's keyboard and ran over the keys to Mr. Craig, tinkling out a funny melody as she ran.

Hi, hi, hi. Sing it again, please!

She had been so good and so quiet for so long, there in Charles's pocket. Bitsy was ready for some fun. After she danced her way across the piano keys to Mr. Craig, she jumped down and ran all around the room, checking everything out. Mr. Craig cracked up when she barked her squeaky bark. "I think that's a high B-flat," he said, playing one of the black keys on the piano keyboard. "No, maybe even a high C." He laughed again. "Has this dog been trained as an opera singer?"

Bitsy jumped back up onto the piano bench, between Charles and Mr. Craig, and looked up at each of them in turn.

Well? When is there going to be more music?

“This is Bitsy,” said Charles. “My family is fostering her. She really loves music—that’s why I had to bring her. I think she wants to hear a song,” said Charles. It sure was lucky that Mr. Craig didn’t seem to be upset about a puppy appearing on his piano. “She really likes that one we were singing. Do you know another one like that?”

Mr. Craig ran his hands over the keys. “How about this?” he asked as his fingers began to dance.

Bitsy sat up straight and wagged her little tail, her head cocked to one side.

I like it. I like it.

Charles joined in as soon as he recognized the song, and they belted it out together. Finally, Mr.

Craig finished with a sweep of his hand up the keys and a happy shout: "woo-hoo!"

Bitsy barked her squeaky bark and wagged her teeny tail. Charles grinned. Who would ever have guessed that piano lessons could be so much fun?

CHAPTER NINE

It was a busy day for music. Mom and Charles got home from his piano lesson just in time to eat a quick dinner before they had to head out again for chorus rehearsal.

Mom was not happy about the way Charles had snuck Bitsy into his piano lesson. She had already let him know that, but she couldn't seem to stop saying it. She lectured him again as they drove to rehearsal.

"You really shouldn't have done that, Charles," said Mom as she pulled into the parking lot of the town hall.

“I know,” said Charles. “But it worked out okay, didn’t it?”

Mom gave him a look in the rearview mirror. “It was still a bad idea to smuggle a puppy into your piano lesson,” she said. “What if Mr. Craig was allergic to dogs, or afraid of them?”

Charles laughed. “Who could be afraid of Bitsy? Maybe a tiny ant or a beetle could, but that’s about it.”

“Just remember to pay attention to what you’re learning,” said Mom as she pulled into a parking spot. “That puppy could be a big distraction.”

Charles nodded. “I promise,” he said.

Just then, Bitsy popped her head out of Charles’s pocket and gave a little squeak.

Me, too!

"What was that?" Mom spun around in her seat. "Charles, you didn't! Don't tell me you brought that puppy to rehearsal."

Charles tried to shoo Bitsy back into his pocket, but she didn't seem to be in the mood for hide-and-seek. "She just loves music so much," he said. "How could I leave her home?"

"Just because Mr. Craig invited you to bring her to the rest of your piano lessons doesn't mean he wants her at rehearsal," Mom said, shaking her head. She blew out a breath. "It's too late to take her home, though. Rehearsal is starting right now, and this is our last practice before the concert. Mr. Craig needs everyone to be here."

Charles encouraged Bitsy back into his pocket. "Go on and hide," he told her. She squirmed into the pocket he was holding open, sticking her head out one more time to give him a sparkly-eyed glance.

Okay, okay. I'll play the game. But somebody better come find me soon!

"She'll be good," Charles promised his mother.

And she was. Mostly.

Bitsy stayed quietly in Charles's pocket as the chorus sang "When You Wish Upon a Star," from the movie *Pinocchio.* She barely moved during "Over the Rainbow." She was as still as a mouse while they sang "Stand by Me." But at the end, when Mr. Craig began to bang out the happy chords for "Do-Re-Mi," she couldn't seem to help herself. Charles felt Bitsy pushing her way out of his pocket. He tried to stop her, but she squirmed her way out and hopped right down onto the riser

Charles was standing on. She stared up at the lines of singers towering over her.

Whoa! This place is full of very big people.

Then she wagged her tail and barked her squeaky-toy bark.

But I can tell that you're all very friendly.

Before Charles could catch her, Bitsy twinkle-toed her way along the riser, weaving in and out between people's feet. She hopped down to the next riser, and the next, and dashed along the floor toward the piano where Mr. Craig sat playing.

By the time she got to Mr. Craig, he had stopped playing and the singers had stopped singing. Everyone was oohing and aahing over Bitsy.

"Is that a dog or a wind-up toy?"

"Look how cute she is!"

"She's adorable!"

Bitsy leapt at Mr. Craig's leg. He reached down to pull her up onto his lap. "Well, well, well," he said. "It looks like we have a very special guest at our rehearsal tonight."

Charles didn't dare to look at Mom. He knew she would be glaring at him. But Mr. Craig seemed fine with having Bitsy there. He gave her a kiss, then got her settled on his lap. "Let's settle down, everyone," he said. "You can all say hi to Bitsy later. Let's get back to what we were working on." He started playing "Do-Re-Mi" again, with Bitsy sitting up straight on his lap, wagging her tiny tail in time to the music.

"Well done," said Mr. Craig, when they got to the end of the song. "I think we're really ready for our show. Congratulations, everyone. We'll see you back here on Saturday night. Don't forget to wear white shirts and black skirts or trousers."

Bitsy squeaked and wagged her tail as she tried to jump up to kiss Mr. Craig on the chin. He laughed, then told the singers they were free to go. "Charles Peterson, would you please stay afterward for a moment?" he finished.

Charles gulped. Was this going to be about Bitsy? He stepped down the risers, with Mom following him. They had to wait until a cluster of singers had drifted away from the piano after petting and praising Bitsy. Finally, Mr. Craig waved Charles forward.

"Is this about bringing Bitsy?" Charles asked. He had decided to jump right in with an apology. "I'm really sorry. I know I shouldn't have."

"Actually, I'm glad you did," said Mr. Craig. "In fact, I think she should come to the show, too. She'll be a real crowd-pleaser."

"Really?" Charles asked. He grinned up at Mom, and she smiled back and shrugged.

"But that's not what I wanted to talk to you about," said Mr. Craig as he handed Bitsy to Charles. "I wanted to ask if you'd help me out at the concert. 'Do-Re-Mi' just doesn't sound right to me anymore unless you're playing the top part. Want to join me?"

CHAPTER TEN

Charles woke up on Saturday, the morning of the concert, to see blue skies outside his window. "Look, Bitsy! It's a beautiful day." He picked up the tiny puppy and held her so she could see.

"Good morning," said Mom at breakfast. "Are you nervous?" she asked, as she handed Charles a bowl of oatmeal with raisins.

He shook his head. "Nope," he said. "Especially since I get to have Bitsy with me."

Mom laughed. "I have a feeling that dog is going to steal the show," she said. "It's so exciting that you're going to be playing piano as well as singing. I'm really proud of you."

"What about you? Are you nervous?" Charles asked Mom.

She laughed. "A little, maybe. But mostly I think it will be fun. Dad and Lizzie and the Bean will be there, and your aunt Amanda, too. They're all going to be so impressed with the way you can sing and play."

Charles ducked his head. "Okay, now I'm nervous," he said.

"Well, you don't need to be. Anyway, you have one more practice with Mr. Craig before tonight's show," Mom reminded him.

"I wish piano lessons weren't ending," said Charles. Mr. Craig was heading home to Kansas the day after the concert, and Charles was going to miss him.

"I think we'll have to find a teacher who lives here," Mom said. "And I've already started looking for a used piano we can buy. Would you like that?"

Charles grinned and nodded. From that moment on, he felt happy all day.

That afternoon he and Mr. Craig laughed and joked through Charles's lesson, and at the end they sang Bitsy's favorite song for her, the one about the brown-eyed girl.

Charles watched the way Mr. Craig was looking at Bitsy as he sang. That's when he knew he had to give up the idea of keeping Bitsy. Bitsy and Mr. Craig belonged together. Who could be a better owner for a music-loving dog?

Charles knew his parents would probably not agree to another dog, anyway. Mom always said that if they adopted a second dog they would have to give up fostering, and nobody was ready for that. It was time to let go of that idea. When the song ended, he took a deep breath and asked the big question. "Mr. Craig, would you like to adopt Bitsy?"

Mr. Craig took his hands off the piano and stared at Charles. "Me? Oh, I don't think so. She's very cute, but I've never had a dog. I travel too much! Anyway, I leave tomorrow, remember? How could I make such a big decision so quickly?"

Charles nodded. "Okay. But please just think about it. Bitsy is the perfect dog for a traveler. She can fit in a pocket, remember?"

That night, Charles and his mom left before the rest of the family, heading to the town hall to get ready for the concert. Mom looked pretty in a lacy white blouse and a black skirt. Charles felt stiff and awkward in his bright white shirt, a red vest, and black pants. Why couldn't he just wear a T-shirt and jeans? Anyway, Bitsy was looking super cute, with a sparkly red ribbon on top of her teeny head. She and Charles had practiced all afternoon how she would sit in his shirt pocket, beneath the red vest, until it was time to come out.

When they walked into the town hall, Charles stopped to stare. Up onstage, the chorus was starting to fill in their spots on the risers. Now Charles understood the white shirt and black pants. The singers looked really professional—like something on TV, not like regular Littleton people. Carrying Bitsy, he headed eagerly down the aisle and climbed up the risers to his place. Everybody he walked by cooed and giggled over Bitsy. "There she is!" he heard someone whisper. "She's so adorable."

Charles thought about it. Everyone who saw

her just loved this tiny puppy. If Mr. Craig wasn't going to adopt Bitsy, who was? Maybe tonight was the perfect opportunity to find her a great home.

Mr. Craig hopped up onto the stage just as Charles found his place. He looked spiffy in a black suit, a white shirt, and a red tie. He was smiling happily. "People," he called, rapping his baton on a music stand, "I just want to say how much fun I've had working with you all. Your enthusiasm and spirit have been so inspiring. Let's show our audience how much we all love to sing tonight, okay?"

That's what they did. At least, Charles thought so. As he sang, he could see faces in the audience smiling back at him: his family, people he knew from school, a cashier from the grocery store.

The concert flew by in a blur. When a song had a sing-along part, the audience sang loudly and cheerfully. Mr. Craig cracked jokes as he introduced each song, and talked about how much he loved Littleton.

Bitsy was so good throughout the whole concert. Charles and Lizzie had tired her out well with an epic game of hide-and-seek, and she lay relaxed in Charles's pocket. He could tell she was enjoying the music—every time he looked down he saw her sparkling eyes—but she didn't jump out of his pocket.

Until it was time for "Do-Re-Mi," Bitsy and Charles's big moment. As soon as Charles worked his way down the risers and sat down on the piano bench next to Mr. Craig, Bitsy popped out and twinkle-toed her way across the keys.

At first, only the people in the front rows could

see. They started to laugh and comment. Then other people started to stand up. The laughter spread, and some people even came down the aisle to get a better look.

Dad jumped up from his seat in the front row. “Want me to take her?” he asked.

Mr. Craig shook his head. “She’s fine,” he said. “She just likes to play her own song before we start.” He put Bitsy up on top of the piano. “Okay, you stay put now, missy,” he told her. He looked at Charles. “Ready?”

“Can I just say something first?” asked Charles. Without waiting for an answer, he took a deep breath and turned to face the audience. “This little puppy is Bitsy, a dog my family is fostering. If you’re interested in adopting her, please talk to me after the concert.”

He turned to Mr. Craig. “Okay, ready,” he said.

His teacher looked shocked—and maybe a

little mad, for the very first time. But he put his hands on the keys and began to play, and Charles joined in. They "rocked that song!" as Lizzie said later. Charles made only one mistake, and it didn't matter because everybody was singing so loudly.

And then the show was over. The chorus took three bows while the audience applauded like crazy, standing up to show how much they'd liked the music. Finally, Mr. Craig hopped up onto the stage to thank everyone for coming.

Some people started to leave—but a flood of others came toward Charles, who still sat on the piano bench. He had Bitsy in his lap, and he was praising her for being so good. When he looked up, there was a crowd around him—all people who might want to adopt Bitsy!

"Excuse me, excuse me, let me through," Charles heard, and suddenly Mr. Craig popped into the middle of the circle. “That dog is not available,” he announced. “I’m adopting her.”

Charles grinned at him. “I guess you thought about it,” he said.

Mr. Craig nodded. “I did. And the answer was obvious. What do you say, Bitsy? Want to come live with me?”

Bitsy sat up and barked her squeaky bark. Her eyes were shining.

You bet I do! Promise to sing for me every day?

Charles felt tears prick at his eyes. It wasn’t easy to let Bitsy go, but he knew that Bitsy and Mr. Craig would be very happy together. “Can we sing her song one more time?” he asked.

“Absolutely,” said Mr. Craig. He pushed back his sleeves, sat down at the piano, and began to play.

La la la-la la-la-la-la la-la-la la-di-dah, sang Charles, along with everyone else who was still in the auditorium. Bitsy danced around on top of the piano. The little brown-eyed girl had found the perfect forever home.

PUPPY TIPS

A tiny dog can be big fun—but a puppy like Bitsy is not the right pet for every household. Very small dogs can be hurt easily, and many "teacup" dogs have health problems. Bitsy's first owners were right to give her up: a family with small, active children is not the best place for a very tiny dog. When your family is ready to adopt a puppy or dog, remember to think about more than just looks. Find a dog that fits your lifestyle. Are you an active family, or are you couch potatoes? Do you have room for a bigger dog, or would a small one be better? Is anyone in the family allergic? Will the dog need grooming? Is the breed good with children and other pets? You can find quizzes online to help you choose your new family member.

Dear Reader,

I took piano lessons when I was Charles's age (my teacher Dorothy used the book *Teaching Little Fingers to Play!*), but I didn't stick with that instrument. When I was in third grade I started to learn to play the flute, and I have been playing ever since. I also love to sing, by myself and with other people, and lately I have come back to playing keyboards. Music has been an important part of my life, and it has brought me a lot of joy over the years. I enjoyed writing about Charles learning to love music the way I do. Do you love music? Do you play an instrument, or sing?

Yours from the Puppy Place,

Ellen Miles

P.S. Sometimes when I sing, my dog, Zipper, howls along with me. It's very funny!

THE PUPPY PLACE

DON'T MISS THE NEXT PUPPY PLACE ADVENTURE!

Here's a peek at Edward

"What do you think of these?" Lizzie Peterson held out a pair of pajamas to show her friend Maria. They were covered in blue and green polka dots and had big purple buttons down the front.

Maria raised her eyebrows. "Very cute," she said. "But I'm not sure they're exactly—'you.'"

Lizzie sighed. None of the pajamas in this store were really "her." "Maybe we should try another store," she said. She saw Maria raise her eyebrows again. Oh, her best friend knew her so well! Maria knew that another store wouldn't make any difference. The fact was, Lizzie was not really a pajama person. She liked to wear a T-shirt and boxer shorts to bed, or a long-sleeved shirt and sweatpants when it was cold. She had never really understood the whole idea of pajamas. Why did you need special clothes for bed? Why couldn't you just wear regular clothes?

"You could just wear a T-shirt and some leggings or something," Maria said.

"Right, and be the only person on Pajamarama Day who's not in pajamas?" Lizzie asked. "I don't think so." Pajamarama was going to be a big deal at Littleton Elementary, where Lizzie and Maria were in fourth grade. Everybody was talking about it already. On the last Friday in September, everybody was going to wear pajamas to school—even the principal, Ms. Guzman, and Mr. Wood, the janitor. Plus, that night the whole fourth grade was going to have a sleepover at school.

Lizzie wasn't even sure why Pajamarama was a thing. It was bad enough that people had special clothes for sleeping—now they were all going to wear them to school? What was the point? She sighed and put the polka-dot pajamas back on the rack. Maybe she should just wear the one pair of pajamas that she did own, the purple ones with a design of little red dogs. She'd had them for years, so they were pretty worn out and they didn't fit perfectly anymore, but at least they were "her." They had dogs on them, and Lizzie was all about dogs.

Lizzie had been dog-crazy for as long as she could remember. Besides the pajamas, she had dog-themed socks, sweatshirts, underpants, and even scrunchies. She had a huge collection of dog books and dog posters. She volunteered at the local animal shelter, helped out at her aunt's doggy daycare, and even had her own very successful dog-walking business. (Maria was one of the partners.) Not only that, she had convinced her parents that their family should foster puppies. That meant that she and her younger brothers, Charles and the Bean, had taken care of dozens of young dogs who needed their help. Every puppy only stayed a little while, until the Petersons found it the perfect forever home.

Well, every puppy but Buddy. Buddy had started out as a foster puppy, but now he was a member of the family. Lizzie loved her little brown puppy more than anything in the world. Knowing that Buddy would always be hers made up for having to say good-bye to all of the other puppies she helped foster. "I wish I could find pajamas with pictures of Buddy on them," she said to Maria now. "Wouldn't that be the best? Especially if they showed the little white heart-shaped spot on his chest."

Maria smiled. "Maybe you can find a website where you could get some made. But probably not in time for Pajamarama."

Lizzie rolled her eyes. "Maybe I just won't go to school on Pajamarama Day," she said.

"Oh, come on," Maria said. "It's going to be fun. Can you imagine what kind of wacky p.j.'s Ms. Guzman will come up with?"

Lizzie knew Maria was right. She went back to flipping through the pajama rack, but lost interest almost right away. "We can come back another day," she said. "There's plenty of time." She headed out of the store, with Maria following her.

They walked up Main Street toward Lucky Dog Books, where they were going to meet Lizzie's mom. The air was crisp and the sky was blue, and Lizzie's spirits lifted right away. The sun felt warm on her face as she strolled down the street.

"Hi, Lizzie," said Mrs. DeMaio, who was sweeping the sidewalk in front of the little grocery store she owned. "How's Buddy?"

"He's great," Lizzie said. She loved it that Buddy was such a celebrity in their town. She wished she had him with her right now. Everybody liked Buddy, and she loved stopping into stores with him for a pet or a biscuit. She knew that Jerry Small, the owner of the bookstore, was a special fan. He would give her a big biscuit to take home to Buddy.

They passed the corner gas station where her dad had once found an abandoned puppy in a cardboard box. "Poor little Snowball," said Lizzie. "I remember when we brought him home. He was so dirty and skinny!" He had been one of the Petersons' first foster puppies, and once they had cleaned him up and fed him, he was one of the cutest—fluffy and white. They had found Snowball a perfect home. Lizzie smiled as she walked along, thinking about it.

Then she saw something that made her lose her smile. She stopped short in the middle of the sidewalk. "Do you see what I see?" she asked Maria. She pointed to the yellow VW Beetle they had just passed, parked in front of the drugstore. The back windows were open, but just barely. A small black puppy stood on the backseat, his front legs up on the car door. His flat, wrinkly nose reached for the crack at the top of the window. He panted hard. His pink tongue hung out, and his bulgy black eyes gave his face a frightened look.

"Poor little pug!" Lizzie said, poking a finger through the window to pet his wet nose. The puppy snuffled at her finger, then gave it a lick. "Argh!" said Lizzie. "This makes me so mad."

ABOUT THE AUTHOR

Ellen Miles loves dogs, which is why she has a great time writing the Puppy Place books. And guess what? She loves cats, too! (In fact, her very first pet was a beautiful tortoiseshell cat named Jenny.) That's why she came up with the Kitty Corner series. Ellen lives in Vermont and loves to be outdoors with her dog, Zipper, every day, walking, biking, skiing, or swimming, depending on the season. She also loves to read, cook, explore her beautiful state, play with dogs, and hang out with friends and family.

Visit Ellen at www.ellenmiles.net.